THE BLACK SHUCK

AND OTHER STORIES

Collins

Contents

Core

Unit 6: The Black Shuck 6
Unit 7: The Meeting Garden 12
Unit 8: The Sharpest Shooters 18
Unit 9: Cosmic Adventure 24
Unit 10: Your Brain: Explained 30

Challenge

Unit 6: I Am Gus 38
Unit 7: Street Art 44
Unit 8: Sports For All 50
Unit 9: Star Spotting 56
Unit 10: Dear Grandma 62

Consolidate

Unit 6: A Dark Wood 70
Unit 7: The Boiling River 76
Unit 8: Sports Jobs 82
Unit 9: Mars Q+A 88
Unit 10: Too Much Sugar 94

Core texts

The Black Shuck

oo	*oo*

people	someone	where	anyone

The Black Shuck is a non-fiction text in the form of a witness report.

Black Shuck, a ghostly black dog that roams the English coasts and countryside of East Anglia, is considered to be a folktale by many people. There are stories of sightings of Black Shuck going back more than a thousand years! But the most **discussed** sighting of this enormous black dog was in 1577, when it attacked a group of villagers who ran into a church for **shelter** from a storm in Bungay, Suffolk. In this **witness** account, you will hear how the **unsuspecting** villagers **attempted** to flee from a terrifying attack by Black Shuck.

Vocabulary:
- **discussed:** talked about
- **shelter:** a place that provides cover (e.g. from bad weather)
- **witness:** someone who was there when an event happened
- **unsuspecting:** not aware of any danger
- **attempted:** tried

What would make you believe that something like the Black Shuck was real?

The Black Shuck

It is a moonlit night in the summer of 1577. A sudden thunderstorm has made people run into a church for shelter. As they wait for the storm to end, something chilling happens ...

A big black dog bursts into the church and attacks!

Many people have discussed what happened that night. This is the record of a witness who was there.

There was a thin moon on that dark night. I had never seen such a terrible storm. It was lashing with monsoon-like rain, and forked flashes of lightning lit up the night.

We hid in the church, candles flickering in the gloom. The mood was dark. All of a sudden, there was a boom of thunder and something sprang into the church. All the candles went out.

A big black dog stood next to me! I scooted further into a dark corner. The dog drooled and shook itself.

Quicker than lightning, the dog swooped upon an unsuspecting man. Someone attempted to fight it off with a broom, but the dog loomed up, snarled and snapped the broom in two.

I was too afraid to look.

Then there was a bright flash and a colossal bang. Lightning had struck the church roof!

We scrambled up and rushed out as part of the roof fell in.

In the churchyard, we were soon soaked to the skin. People were wailing and yelling. Where was the dog? I turned and looked, but it had vanished into the night ...

People called the dog 'Black Shuck'.

There have been further sightings of Black Shuck in this part of England. If anyone sees Black Shuck, it is said to bring doom and disaster.

Are the reports of Black Shuck facts? Perhaps not, but look at these scorch marks in the wood from the church.

Did a dog do this with its nails? Is it proof that Black Shuck was there?

What do you think?

The Meeting Garden

| ow | oi |

| friends | woman | said | made | where |

The Meeting Garden is a contemporary story.

The Meeting Garden may have been **neglected** and even **unkempt**, but for Tamsin, Makena and their friends it was a special place to meet and relax. But one awful day the friends discover that the Meeting Garden is under threat from **developers** who want to **construct** new homes. The friends find out that their garden is on **brown land** and so they decide to persuade the town council that the Meeting Garden is worth saving.

Vocabulary:
- **neglected:** not properly cared for
- **unkempt:** messy and a bit wild
- **developers:** a company that builds houses or other buildings
- **construct:** build
- **brown land:** land that has been used before and so can be built on

Is there a place that is special to you? What do you like to do there?

THE MEETING GARDEN

In a run-down part of town, there was a neglected strip of grass and bushes. Twisting footpaths led to an unkempt garden shooting up from the rocks and soil. Adults seemed to avoid it, but for Tamsin, Makena and their friends, it was the perfect spot to hang out. They called it the Meeting Garden, and spent a long time chatting there after school.

But one summer afternoon, something shocking happened. Down at the Meeting Garden, a big brown digger was scooping up the soil! Tamsin and Makena asked the woman in the cab what was happening. She said that developers were planning to put houses on the garden.

For Tamsin and Makena, this was a disaster.

"We can't let them spoil the garden!" said Tamsin, frowning.

Makena made a vow. "This isn't good, but if we join together we can fight it."

So the next morning at school, they planned.

"I'll ask my mum to call the tabloids," said Makena.

"I'll look up the developers to book an appointment," said Tamsin.

Their friends joined in to make banners, and a big crowd of them went to the meeting with the developers.

The developers said the Meeting Garden was 'brown land', so they were allowed to construct houses there.

Tamsin and Makena stood up. "We've downloaded this map," said Tamsin.

Makena pointed out the Meeting Garden. "Look, the garden's the greenest part of town!"

"The point is, we love this garden," added Tamsin. "It's the one spot in town where we can relax and hang out."

The crowd were soon clapping and hooting.

One week on, Tamsin and Makena got a letter from the town planners. It said that the developers were not allowed to construct houses on the Meeting Garden after all. The letter said:

> Thank you for pointing out that this garden is too important to spoil. It can remain the Meeting Garden forever.

"That's so cool!" said Tamsin. "We did it – together!"

The Sharpest Shooters

air	ear

who's	don't	very	because	time

The Sharpest Shooters is a graphic novel.

It's the beginning of the season and the Sharpest Shooters have **gathered** for their first practice session. Coach Cora has a simple plan to move up the **rankings**: win from the start and don't stop winning! Faith is a **fresh** face on the team, and she wants to impress Coach Cora. But when the team play their first game of the season, the polished floor causes problems. The players can't concentrate because their trainers make an awful **screeching** sound that makes them feel like their **ears are bleeding**! The Sharpest Shooters need someone with **flair** to take them to victory. Is that person Faith?

Vocabulary:
- **gathered:** got people together in one place
- **rankings:** positions of teams in a league table
- **fresh:** brand-new
- **screeching:** a high-pitched sound
- **ears are bleeding:** when a high-pitched sound hurts your ears
- **flair:** doing something really well in an original way

What do you enjoy more: doing sport or watching sports? Why?

The Sharpest Shooters

The Sharpest Shooters moved up the rankings last year, but they are not in the clear – yet. This year, they need to win right from the start and keep on winning. Coach Cora has gathered them to meet and make a plan.

Coach Cora brings training to an end. The Sharpest Shooters are cooling down but gossip is hanging in the air.

One week on, the Sharpest Shooters are at the club. They are up against the All Stars. But the fresh polish on the wood seems to be a problem …

My ears are bleeding from the screeching of our trainers!

The wood is too smooth now! I'm afraid to run because I think I'll slip. This is unfair!

Block her, Bella!

What? I can't hear you!

SCREECH!

Don't despair! We can get past this and win!

There is no time for fear. The Sharpest Shooters have to get into gear.

The power of the All Stars is clear! The Sharpest Shooters can't get near to the hoop ...

... we need to see some flair from the Sharpest Shooters now if they want to win!

Faith appears out of thin air to slam dunk ...

Go on, Faith!

Cosmic Adventure

/n/ kn   /ch/ tch ture

water   our   something   through

Cosmic Adventure is a science-fiction graphic novel.

Blair and Mitch are travelling through space, looking for planets that might be **inhabited**. They hope they can learn about the habitats and **cultures** on these planets. But on this mission things don't go as planned and they crash-land, cracking the **structure** of their rocket. Not wanting to waste a chance to explore, Blair and Mitch **venture** out and soon come across **exotic** animals and plants. But when something **latches** onto Mitch's leg, they **scratch** all thoughts of exploration in a desperate bid to escape!

Vocabulary:
- **inhabited:** when animals, people or other living things live somewhere
- **cultures:** the ideas, behaviours and beliefs of a group of people or society
- **structure:** the frame of an object or building
- **venture:** to go on a risky journey
- **exotic:** unusual; out of the ordinary
- **latches:** grabs hold of tightly
- **scratch:** to cancel or abandon something

What do you think will be the biggest danger that Blair and Mitch face?

COSMIC ADVENTURE

Blair and Mitch are on a cosmic adventure. They have ventured deep into the cosmos looking for inhabited planets. They want to gain an understanding of different cultures.

We are fearless ... !

You might be, but I admit that I'm a bit afraid.

Did you feel that, Mitch?

The monitors are glitching. It appears that we were knocked by a comet. Hang on tight!

The rocket crashes down onto a planet. Mitch and Blair are hurled into the air. They are scratched and in shock but not hurt. Mitch fetches their helmets.

The cosmic adventure is on! Mitch and Blair trek down a twisting path that stretches into a dark forest. Exotic animals hiss and snarl. Blair records it all.

"Cosmic adventure record 1. This planet is inhabited. The level of risk is unclear. For now, we will just collect pictures and remain near our rocket."

Blair spots a flashing insect and sets off to inspect it. Mitch is kneeling down to get a picture as Blair disappears.

All of a sudden, a pink serpent uncoils and springs out from a patch of darkness. It catches the insect. Mitch is startled and stumbles. He stretches out to grab a branch, but he misses and lands splat in the pond.

Blair! Help! Get here, now! Something is twisting up my legs! It has latched onto my knees. It's going to drag me under!

Your Brain: Explained

| /r/ wr | /w/ wh | /f/ ph |

| many | friends | thoughts | because |

Your Brain: Explained is a non-fiction text in the form of a quiz.

All of our brains are unique. We have unique strengths and challenges too. This quiz helps you to get to know your **phenomenal** brain a bit better. Find out if you prefer to do things at speed, if you prefer fun and **impractical** solutions or if you like careful planning rather than making a quick **sketch** and having a go! These **assorted** questions will help you realise just how **flexible** your brain is … and how incredible you are!

Vocabulary:
- **phenomenal:** incredible
- **impractical:** not very sensible or easy to use
- **sketch:** a quick drawing
- **assorted:** lots of different things put together
- **flexible:** ready and able to change

Have you ever thought about how you think and do things? What do you love doing the most?

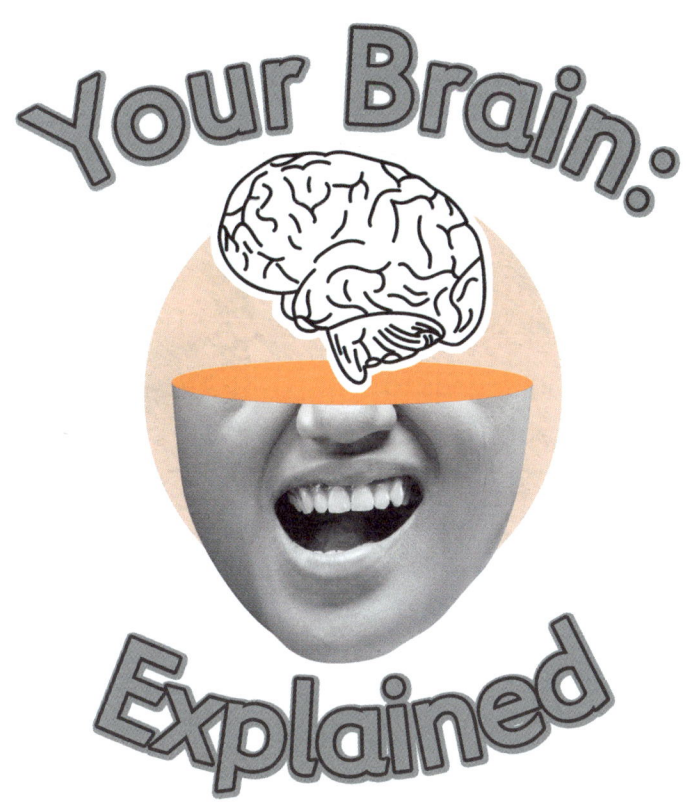

Your Brain: Explained

Have you ever considered how phenomenal your brain is? It helps you do so many things. But all brains are different. How you think, feel and tackle problems differs according to how your brain works.

Are you a whizz at puzzles? Do you have a knack for knitting? Hard to catch on the pitch? Or is your strength whipping up a dazzling dinner?

This quiz will help you understand how your brain works. Pick the letter that fits you best.

1 When there's a problem, what do you do?
  A. Have a go. Getting things wrong is fun!
  B. Whip up an impractical plan!
  C. Approach it step by step.
  D. Whizz through it!
  E. Chat with friends to work it out.
  F. Seek out fresh air to get your thoughts in order.

2 What do you do when it's raining?
  A. Attempt a difficult puzzle.
  B. Make a wrap filled with assorted foods!
  C. Sort out your bedroom.
  D. Twitch – you dislike being still!
  E. Hang out with friends.
  F. Fetch an umbrella and go on an adventure.

3 You are given a big task. How do you start?

A. Make a complex written plan.

B. Think of an interesting approach and sketch a picture of it.

C. Split the job into simple steps.

D. Start at whichever bit you like best.

E. Ask friends to help you.

F. Go into the fresh air, then begin.

4 When do you feel content?

A. Tackling a problem or puzzle.

B. Sketching, singing, cooking!

C. When problems are sorted out.

D. Whizzing from task to task.

E. Chatting with friends.

F. Chilling in the garden.

Results

Lots of As: You like cracking puzzles and spotting clever fixes.

Lots of Bs: You are artistic and good at inventing things.

Lots of Cs: You are methodical and put an emphasis on sorting things out.

Lots of Ds: You are a fast thinker, often working at high speed.

Lots of Es: You like working with people.

Lots of Fs: You love plants and animals and work best in the fresh air.

Was it sometimes difficult to pick a letter? That's because a quiz cannot tell you the whole picture. Our brains have a mixture of traits which help us to be flexible thinkers.

For example, you might be an expert at understanding people's feelings, and work best when you are with friends. But you might need time by yourself, too.

Or you might get a buzz from doing thrilling things, like swimming near dolphins. But when you sit still and do something relaxing like sketching, you might get a similar buzz.

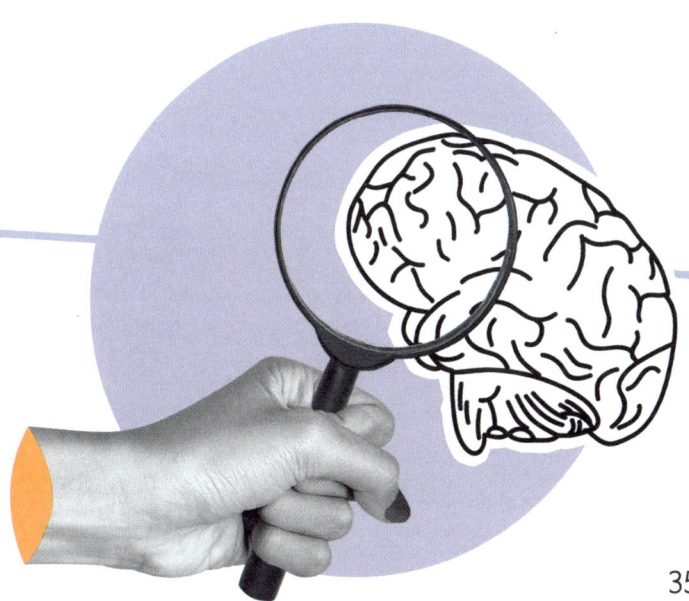

Challenge texts

I Am Gus

oo	oo

asked	move	there

I Am Gus is a spooky story set in a supermarket. It is told in the first person.

A simple trip to the supermarket to buy some beetroot for dinner becomes a terrifying experience when Gus, the strangest supermarket employee ever, offers to 'help'.

In this **unsettling** story, Gus appears just as the narrator has **prodded** and **selected** the beetroot they want. Gus behaves in a very unsettling way: **chanting** and dancing, while wearing one **tattered** boot. The narrator is **transfixed** with terror. Will they be able to get free of Gus? Or will we find out how Gus 'helps' them?

Vocabulary:
- **unsettling:** making you feel anxious or uneasy
- **prodded:** poked with your fingers
- **selected:** chosen
- **chanting:** speaking in a sing-song voice
- **tattered:** worn down and falling apart
- **transfixed:** unable to move

Is there any ordinary thing or place that you find scary or unsettling?

I AM GUS

Mum asked me to go and get a beetroot. She was cooking dinner.

I get that it looks odd, but when I get fresh food from the shop, I prod it to check if it's good. Like ... with a beetroot, if it's too soft it will turn to disgusting goop between your fingers.

That morning, things started off as normal. The shop was chilled out.

I looked at the beetroots, prodded the good-looking ones, then selected the best beetroot – simple.

But then, I looked up, turned and spotted him.

A man loomed next to me. He looked right at me.

"Step back, man!" I said.

He looked like he was from the past. Skin like a rotting apple. He smelled like damp mud.

I visit this shop often, but I had never seen him. He had a lanyard drooping from his neck - it said: **'I Am Gus, Let Me Help'**.

I wiggled the beetroot at him. "Look! No help needed —"

The man didn't move.

But then his lips curled into a crooked grin.

"Are you OK ... Gus?" I asked.

What happened next shook me up. He started hopping from foot to foot, still grinning. He swooshed his too-long arms left and right, in an unsettling jig. He bashed into the shelf – a pack of mushrooms fell.

He stopped jigging. My chest tightened.

He took the mushrooms, ripped the pack, and started hurling handfuls of mushrooms at himself. They landed on him, like sprinkles on a muffin.

My legs felt like rocks – I was transfixed with terror.

His grin got bigger. He took a tattered boot off. Just the left boot. He lifted it high and slipped his hand into it.

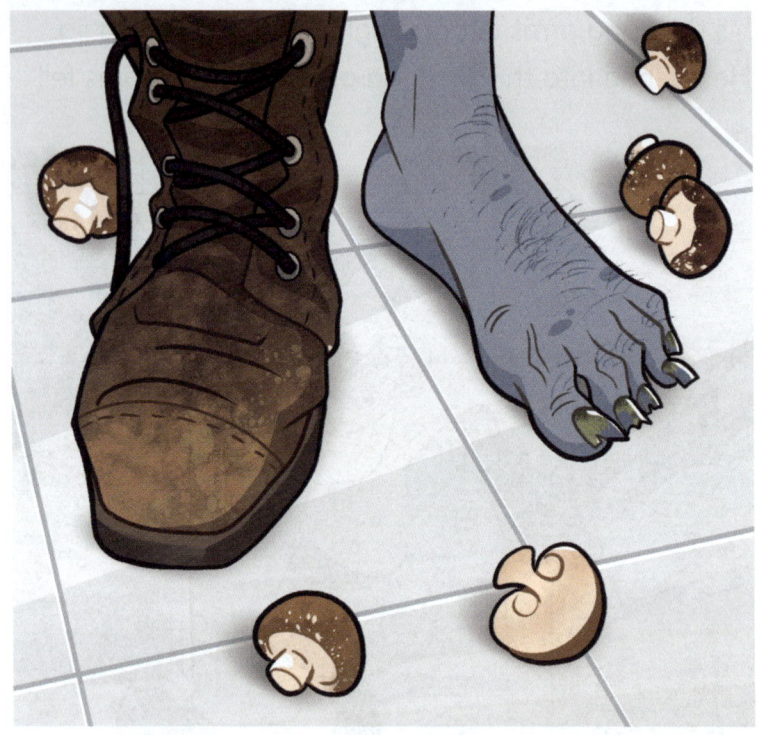

Then his jig quickened. His booted foot stomped and his bootless, sockless foot slapped.

STOMP! SLAP! Quicker!

He shook the stinking boot at me like a horrid puppet and chanted, "Fun Gus! Fun Gus!"

The boot dropped off his hand, and landed next to his feet.

His lips drooped. A sickening look.

Then he SPRINTED.

A burst of arms and legs dashed at me. I gripped my beetroot tight in terror. I yelled at the top of my lungs.

"NOOOOOO!"

Then ... he vanished. No boot. No mushrooms. No Gus.

The shop was back to normal.

I chucked 50p at the till and darted to the exit.

But ... he was there, too!

"Did you have fun?" Gus snarled.

Street Art

ow	oi

whole	houses	because	people

Street Art is a non-fiction text.

There is a type of art that is free to everyone – street art! You have probably seen **tags** and other graffiti on buildings. This is made by street artists who want to express their ideas out in the open. Street artists **transform** buildings into art. Some artists work together; others prefer a more individual **approach**. Street art has become an attraction, bringing visitors to cities like Manchester (UK) to find the bee **emblem** in the art that decorates the city. Street artists often work with communities to celebrate what makes that place unique. Find out about artists who have created art to join people across the **continents**.

Street artists create art with permission from property owners or through official community projects.

Vocabulary:
- **tags:** the stylised signature or logo of a graffiti artist
- **transform:** to completely change something
- **approach:** a way of doing something
- **emblem:** a symbol that shows an important quality about a person or place
- **continents:** Africa, Antarctica, Asia, Australia, Europe and North and South America

Would you prefer to see art outside or in a gallery?

Not all art is like this.

This is street art. It is out on the street, so we can all see it for free.

This painting is bursting with monsters!

You might spot art down a street in your town. Street art comes in many different forms, from tags and stickers to whole houses being painted. Street art paintings are often big and can have a lot of impact.

Landmarks

This painting is called 'Six Sisters' because six women joined together to paint a street of shops in Bristol, UK. The artists all took a different approach to painting the shops. From pink dogs frolicking in sunflowers, to bees on a bright backdrop, the effect is powerful. They transformed a plain street into a landmark.

One artist didn't stop with just one street. He cloaked his town with a burst of bright paintings. Thanks to this street art, the town is now a top sightseeing spot that attracts crowds of visitors.

What can street art tell us?

The subject matter of street art can link to where it is. For example, lots of street art in Manchester, UK, contains bees because the bee is the emblem of Manchester.

This painting, in Scotland, points out that Scotland gets green power from windmills. This painting is part of a street art trail.

Portraits

Many street art paintings are portraits. A portrait is a painting of a person.

This towering portrait is of a cook. It seems like he's looking out at people on the street. How do you think he's feeling? It looks like he's frowning – perhaps he's sad that he needs to boil the lobster!

In Brazil, you can see one of the longest street art paintings by one artist. It has stunning portraits from all continents, joined to look like a bright quilt. The artist explained that the painting tells us, 'We are all connected.'

Joint projects

Some street art is painted by lots of artists. It can be a project for the people in a town to join in with.

This painting, in the US, was a joint project by an artist and 14 teens. The artist said, 'Art is for all of us.'

Big, bright art like this is called Pop Art. It looks like a cartoon, with its strong black borders and bright scarlets and greens.

Pop Art started in the 1950s. Artists often painted normal objects, like food cans and people, but they made them look vivid and dramatic.

Look out for street art in your town!

Sports For All

air	ear

would	through	water	people

Sports for All is a non-fiction text.

Find out how sports can be **adapted** to include everyone. With the help of **adjusted** sports **gear**, disabled surfers have broken records. And disabled sailors like Natasha Lambert have **accomplished** record-breaking voyages. She sails on a **sip-and-puff boat** that she steers using her breath! You'll be amazed at the fearlessness of bobsledders who use a **4-point harness** to strap themselves into tiny sleds and hurtle down **hairpin bends**.

Vocabulary:
- **adapted:** changed in some way
- **adjusted:** changed to make it more suitable
- **gear:** the equipment you need for a sport
- **accomplished:** succeeded at a challenge
- **sip-and-puff boat:** an adapted boat used by people with disabilities affecting their hands and limbs
- **4-point harness:** a system with two shoulder straps and two lap straps that holds a person in place
- **hairpin bends:** very tight corners

What sport that takes you out of your comfort zone would you like to try?

SPORTS FOR ALL

What's your go-to sport? Would you prefer shooting down river rapids in a raft or hurtling down a freezing bobsled track with the air zipping past your ears? Are you a fan of hair-raising sports like BMXing, or perhaps sailing floats your boat?

You'll be delighted to hear that loads of top sports can be adapted so we can all join in.

"How?" I hear you ask.

Well, sometimes the gear is adjusted, and sometimes the sport is adapted so it is fair.

Surfing

Surfing must be one of the coolest sports, right? If you are near the coast and like to feel the wind in your hair, this might be the sport for you!

Some surfers sit on a chair. A surf instructor swims at the back and helps them move through the water. Look at this pair working together!

Smashing records!

Matt Formston has the record for the highest ever para surf. He surfed a crest that was 15.48 m high. That's as high as 4 buses! Matt has less than 3% of his sight. It's clear that he is fearless!

Bobsledding

Bobsledders sit in sleds with steel runners, then shoot down a steep track, twisting and turning through hairpin bends. The track is chilled to −11°C so that water freezes in a thin, smooth sheet. This is perfect for bobsleds to speed down!

It's common to have 2–4 people in a bobsled. However, adapted bobsleds are often just for one person. They might be adapted to have a 4-point harness to strap the bobsledder in, or a one-handed rod to handle the sled.

Bobsledders need the right gear. A bobble hat and a pair of earmuffs will not cut it! They need a Kevlar vest and helmet to protect them if they crash.

Sailing

Ever hear of a sip-and-puff boat? This incredible boat can be sailed by a person sipping air in and puffing air out. If you sip, the boat turns right. If you puff, the boat turns left. Clever! You can adjust the sails, too.

Smashing records!

In 2020, Natasha Lambert sailed across the Atlantic with flair on a sip-and-puff boat. No one had accomplished this until then.

Powerlifting

Powerlifters do three different lifts – two standing and one sitting.

Powerlifting can be adapted so people just do one sort of lift. They do the bench press. They lift a loaded bar clear off a rack, to their chest, then back up in the air. A referee stands near the powerlifter to check the contest is fair. The powerlifter must lock their arms until the referee says: "Rack."

Year on year, the number of people joining clubs with adapted sports gets bigger. Did one light a spark in you?

Star Spotting

| /n/ kn | /ch/ tch ture |

| people | because | once | move |

Star Spotting is a non-fiction text.

People have told stories about the stars throughout human history. Every **culture** has tales to tell us about the stars. **Astronomers** study space and the stars. They **capture** information about the stars in star maps. They can predict which stars come into our view by plotting the **orbit** of the Earth around the sun. Even now, sailors and **NASA** use these maps to **plot** their routes.

Discover how you can **detect** constellations and find your way at night by spotting Polaris, the North Star.

Vocabulary:
- **culture:** the ideas, behaviours and beliefs of a group of people or society
- **astronomers:** people who study space, stars and the universe
- **capture:** to record in words or pictures
- **orbit:** path of a spacecraft, star, moon or planet as it moves around another bigger planet, moon or star
- **NASA:** National Aeronautics and Space Administration; the American space agency
- **plot:** plan out
- **detect:** find

Why do you think NASA needs star maps?

Star Spotting

Pictures in the stars

People from all cultures have looked up at night and spotted patterns in the stars. They have connected the stars into vast join-the-dots pictures of animals, objects and people, like hunters and knights. If you look up on a clear night, you might detect some of these pictures.

What stars can you see?

You will see different stars depending on where you are on the planet. The stars you can spot depends on the time of year, too. This is because our planet orbits the sun (a very important star!) once a year. So, from one night to the next, the patch of stars we see is a little different.

Star maps

To us, it appears that the stars move but in fact they remain still. In the past, astronomers mapped the stars to capture where they are. These star maps helped sailors plot their paths on their adventures. Today, NASA still has star maps as a backup.

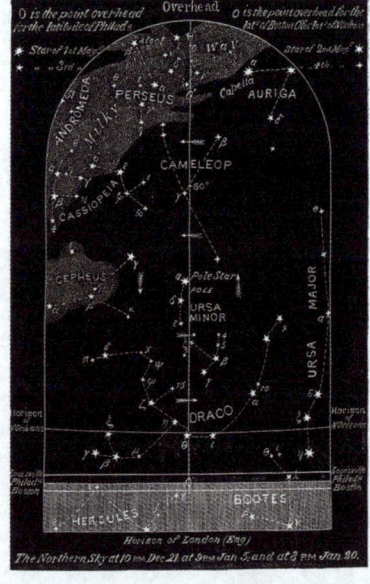

What star pictures can you spot?

On a clear night, you might spot an assortment of pictures in the stars, for example:

The Big Dipper

The Big Dipper is an asterism, a term for a pattern of stars. It consists of seven bright stars that, when joined together, are said to match a picture of a big dipping spoon.

The brightest star in the Big Dipper is 100 times brighter than the sun!

Different cultures call this asterism different things.

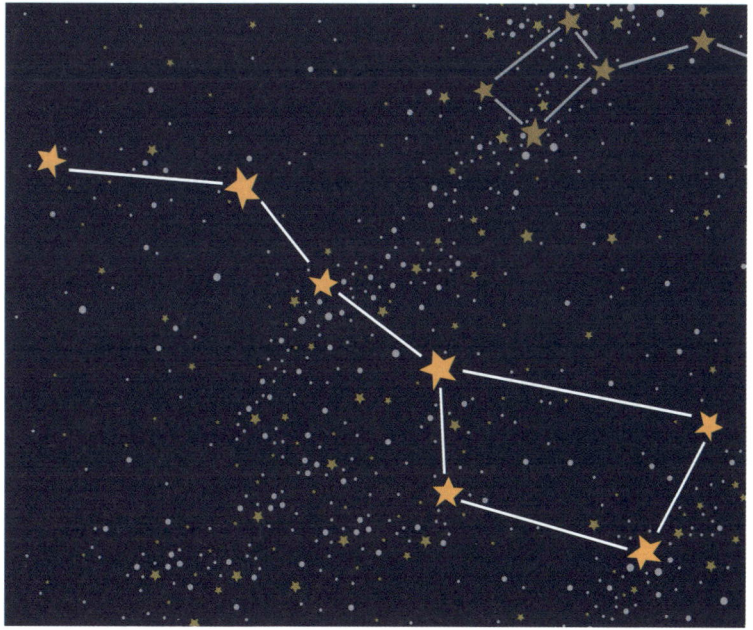

The Kneeling Man

This cluster of stars is often pictured as a man kneeling down on one knee, with an arm stretched in the air. His foot rests on top of a nearby cluster of stars that represents a dragon.

The Kneeling Man was recorded in a book by an astronomer in 150 CE.

You can catch sight of the Kneeling Man in the summer in the UK.

Star-spotting tips:

1) Pick the clearest night possible to avoid disappointment.

2) Avoid a spot with too much light. Switching off lights is important – the darker the better! Stars are clearest on a pitch-black night.

3) You can download a star-spotting app. But if you have an app, put your screen on the night setting to lessen the light.

4) Polaris is called the North Star because it points north at all times. If you can spot it, you can tell where north is. It can help you to pinpoint the Big Dipper, too, as this is near to Polaris.

5) See where the sun is setting. That is west. From this, you can tell where north is and that will help you with spotting stars.

6) Capture what you see. Have a go at sketching the stars, then 'join the dots' to form patterns.

Dear Grandma

/r/ wr	/w/ wh	/f/ ph

would	thought	people	today

Dear Grandma is a story in the form of letters.

Hannah's grandma has dementia: she is losing her memory and worries that she's a **burden**. Hannah writes to her grandma to remind her of happy memories. Hannah begins with a letter about a time when she waited impatiently, through a **Torah** reading, for the blast of a ram's horn trumpet to signal the end of **Yom Kippur**. She writes about spinning the **sevivon** to win **Hannakah gelt**, the **matza** they shared during the holiday Passover, and the **hallah** they ate on **Shabbat**.

Vocabulary:
- **burden:** something that causes worry or difficulty
- **Torah:** the first part of the Jewish bible
- **Yom Kippur:** a Jewish holiday when people ask for forgiveness and don't eat for 25 hours
- **sevivon:** a spinner used in a game
- **Hannakah gelt:** chocolate coins (Note: there are many English spelling variations for the word Hannakah. We have used the version that is easiest to code.)
- **matza:** a flatbread made with flour and water
- **hallah:** a loaf of bread made with eggs
- **Shabbat:** Saturday, a day of rest when Jewish people worship and spend time with their families

What food do you share when you celebrate?

Dear Grandma

When Dad said that Grandma was not going to get better, I wept. He said she would stop remembering things and might forget us too. I might have been shocked, but Grandma was the picture of despair. She thought the doctor was wrong, but deep down she understood what was happening.

From then on, she remembered the past better than the present. Things that had just happened were lost to her. Grandma and I would look at pictures together in her kitchen but sometimes she got things wrong. So, I thought I would send her letters, which would be a written record of important people and events for her.

Dear Grandma,

Do you remember Yom Kippur when I was eleven? We didn't have any food from sunset to sunset. We sat together to hear the Torah. I got bored and wriggled.

You patted me on the knee and whispered, "It's hard not to wriggle. Quick, creep out and stretch your legs. Come back when you are wriggle-free!"

When I returned, the blast of the ram's horn at the end was ear-splitting.

We ended the fast at your house with a big supper. You picked toast to end your fasts, but Dad prefers pickles. I switched to toast to be like you. Toast seems just right when you are famished!

Love Hannah

Dear Grandma,

Do you remember when it was Hannakah, the festival of lights? We lit candles and spun the sevivon. I got lots of Hannakah gelt from it. I took off the wrappers and munched them all up, and was not far from being sick!

You cooked latkes and we sat and sang in the kitchen with the candles alight on the shelf. It got dark and the candles burned bright – it was so snug. Whenever I think of that night, I think of how Dad got you that comical menorah, which looked like an elephant! We must light it again this year.

Love Hannah

Dear Grandma,

Do you remember the last time we had matza? We swept the house looking for any specks of food that we shouldn't have, and you cooked for sixteen people. I whisked up a dessert from nuts and eggs and you said it was perfect.

Uncle Josh tripped and spilled his food. I whizzed off to clear it up. I could see then that you were ill. Grandpa looked sad and you said similar things a lot of times.

Love Hannah

Dear Grandma,

Today is Shabbat. We will come to your house and sit in the kitchen when Grandpa finishes cooking the roast chicken. Then we will light the candles and have hallah and the blessings. Have you remembered it is Shabbat?

You said you feel as if you are a burden. But you are not. You are my perfect Grandma. You still dress like a queen, and we love you so much.

I have captured all I remember and written it for you. Whenever you look at my letters, remember just how fantastic you are!

Love Hannah

Consolidate texts

A Dark Wood

oo	oo

through	move	any

A Dark Wood is a rhyming poem.

This spooky poem is written from the point of view of someone who enjoys the thrill of being in the woods at night. They are **expectant** as they travel through the moonlit woods and are **alert** to the sounds of the night. The moonlight **uncloaks** the woods and as the traveller's sight **adjusts**, they see the trees **slick** with rain, moths' wings **unfurl**, and the beauty of the wood at night is revealed.

But something catches the poet's eye and then they hear a **muffled** thud … they are not alone.

Vocabulary:
- **expectant:** excited about something that is about to happen
- **alert:** tuned in to notice things
- **uncloaks:** uncovers
- **adjusts:** becomes used to something
- **slick:** wet and slippery
- **unfurl:** spread out
- **muffled:** a soft sound

What would tempt you to go on a walk in the woods at night?

A Dark Wood

Afternoon turns from dusk to night,
And I thrill with shivers of delight.

The mood shifts as night creeps in,
I'm alert as the light gets dim.

Monsoon rains hammer and thud,
Churning up the soaking mud.

Winds strain and groan as water pools
By slick tree roots and red toadstools.

Drumming rain and dripping bark
Is all I see in the endless dark.

Looming trees mutter as I slip through,
They seem to gossip in the gloom.

The deep groan of a crooked oak,
The drip of rain, the softest croak.

A hooting call in the dark,
Moonlit dogs begin to bark.

My footsteps disturb the expectant wood,
Moonlight uncloaks me, this isn't good.

As my sight adjusts to the dark,
I begin to see things move and dart.

Moths unfurl, flutter and zoom,
Flitting past the cool, bright moon.

Screeching bats loop and dip,
Seeking insects that flit and zip.

But soon I feel it's not just me ...
Is there someone here, could it be?

Then I see footprints in the mud,
And what is that? A muffled thud?

Then the flash of a bright red hood,
Dashing through the dark, wet wood.

A woman darts and then turns to look,
She's like a person from a book!

With black boots and a trailing cloak,
She hurtles past a crooked oak.

By myself again with just the rain,
My senses sharp as they seek and strain.

I stop to look at the trees and bracken,
Was she there? Did any of it happen?

The Boiling River

ow	oi

because	sometimes	water	through

The Boiling River is a non-fiction text about part of the Amazon.

Find out about a river that you would NOT like to dip your toe into! The Boiling River **drifts** through the Peruvian Amazon. It is heated by **magma** that has escaped through the earth's **mantle**. This extraordinary river is free of any **contaminants** and is safe to drink, once it is cool! This **distinct** habitat is being researched by scientists so that they can gain **insights** into what could happen to other rivers if the earth continues to heat up.

Vocabulary:
- **drifts:** moves slowly
- **magma:** extremely hot melted rock
- **mantle:** an incredibly thick layer of rock between the earth's super-heated core and its crust
- **contaminants:** things that are polluting or poisonous
- **distinct:** different and special
- **insights:** deep understanding

Why might the Boiling River be an interesting place to visit?

THE BOILING RIVER

Mists drift down a hill to where a boiling river is hidden in a rift in the Amazon rainforest. If you stand on its brown soil banks and look down, you will not see any living things in it. This is because the river's boiling waters kill all the plants and any animal that has the bad luck to slip in. It is not drowning that will kill them, but being cooked.

La Bomba

The hottest part of the Boiling River is a hot spring called La Bomba that is 97°C. Sometimes the spring gets as hot as 99°C – just one degree from boiling point.

The spring is made by water that has been boiled by magma that is next to the planet's mantle. As the water boils, it shoots up through cracks in the rocks and soil.

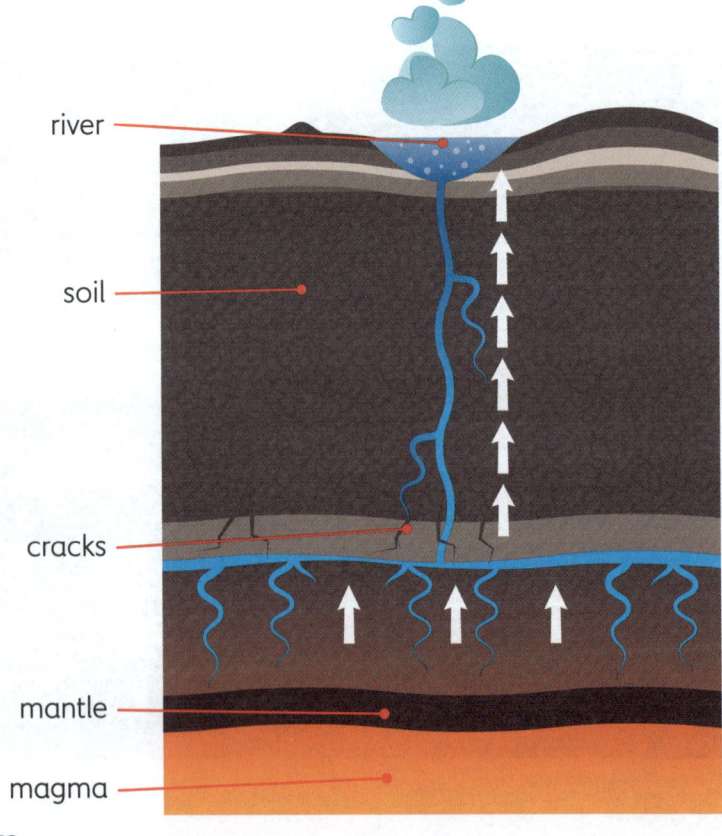

Yacumama

Some people think that a spirit serpent called Yacumama made the river boil. They drink the water to connect to the spirit's power. The water is good to drink because it has been boiled.

But this is all at risk, as the towering trees along the river are being cut down. People are joining together to protect the forest, the river and the animals along it. Animals such as poison dart frogs and screech owls could go extinct, as logging spoils their habitat.

It is important to understand this distinct habitat. Experts collect samples from up and down the river to pinpoint the levels of metals and particles in the water. Now, they have proof that the river is free of contaminants, but they don't yet understand how this occurs.

The Boiling River is an example of how rivers might be affected if the planet isn't kept cool. As understanding deepens, we gain insights into how we should look after our planet.

Sports Jobs

air	ear

who	people	women	don't

Sports Jobs is a non-fiction text in the form of a report.

In this article, Keara interviews three people who have jobs in the world of sport. Each interview **spotlights** the work of **referees**, **medics** and **coaches** and explores the highs and lows of their jobs. The interviews don't **airbrush** the hard work needed to succeed. But you might be surprised which jobs require **degree**-level training and which you can learn on the job.

Vocabulary:
- **spotlights:** gives attention to something
- **referees:** officials who watch the game closely to check the rules are followed
- **medics:** people who are medically trained
- **coaches:** people who train sportsmen and women
- **airbrush:** make something look perfect
- **degree:** a qualification you get at university

Which of these jobs do you think might suit you?

SPORTS JOBS

By Keara Fairburn, reporter

Do you like sports?

Want to get out of your chair?

Keen to help the stars who appear on our screens?

Well, I have just the jobs for you! This article spotlights jobs in sport, from referees to medics to coaches.

Referee

I'm joined by Clair, an expert referee.

Keara: What is your job?

Clair: I check that things are fair.

Keara: Do you like being a referee?

Clair: I love it! However, I'm not going to airbrush what I do. It can be hard when people get cross.

Keara: What skills do you need?

Clair: I must be clear, as it's important that the sportswomen hear me. I need to be fit, too.

Medic

Fern is a skilled sports medic.

Keara: How did you train to be a medic?

Fern: I did a degree and then further training. It was a lot of work but I love sport, so this job is perfect for me.

Keara: How do you handle stress?

Fern: Well, it can get dramatic. Once we had to airlift someone out. But I have to appear cool!

Keara: What's the best bit?

Fern: Being near to the sports stars! Appearing when we are needed to fix their sprains and strains.

Coach

Carl is a coach for a top tennis star.

Keara: I hear this past year has been interesting!
Carl: Well, I went from tennis star to tennis coach ... and now I train winners!
Keara: Wow! And what makes a good coach?
Carl: You can't appear to be stressed – that will not get the best results.
Keara: Any extra pointers?
Carl: Yes, look for fear in your trainees. Do they hang back when they need to get near to the net? Help them make that fear disappear and you'll have a winner!

Thanks to Clair, Fern and Carl!

Did being a referee, medic or coach stand out for you?

If not, don't despair. Keep looking – the right job might appear!

Mars Q+A

| /n/ kn | /ch/ tch ture |

| called | because | water | today |

Mars Q+A is a non-fiction text.

We call Mars the Red Planet, but is it really red? Find out the answer to this and other questions in *Mars Q+A*.

You can't **hitch a lift** to visit Mars (yet) but **NASA** and other space agencies exploring the planet with robots and roamers have discovered where the water that once formed **canyons** has gone. Water is vital for any human settlement on the Red Planet. Spacecrafts that **orbit** the planet gather data about habitats on Mars. Imagine a future when you open the **hatch** from your **living habitat** and take off on your hovercraft to explore!

Vocabulary:
- **hitch a lift:** get a ride in a vehicle
- **NASA:** stands for the National Aeronautics and Space Administration; the American space agency
- **canyons:** deep valleys made through river erosion
- **orbit:** move in a curved path around another larger planet, moon or star
- **hatch:** a strong door that can be sealed so that air does not escape
- **living habitat:** a structure that supports human life

What would you like to know about Mars?

Mars Q+A

Q. Is Mars red?

A. Mars is called the Red Planet. But in pictures sent back from Mars, we can see patches of pink, brown, red and green.

Mars appears red to us because the red dust sent up by winds on Mars catches sunlight. This is what makes the Red Planet so hard to miss.

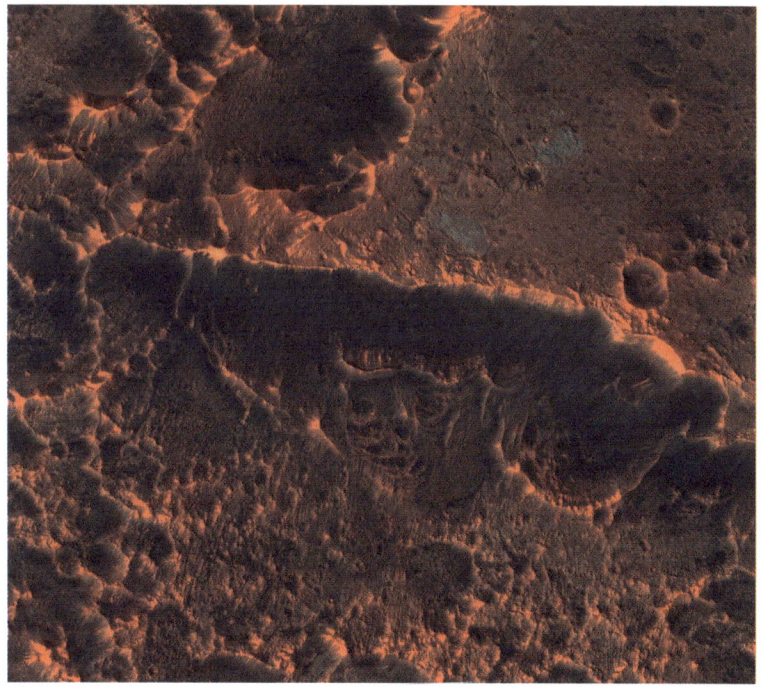

Q. Was there ever water on Mars?

A. Yes, roamers and landers have sent NASA pictures of riverbeds and canyons that were formed by running water.

Riverbeds stretch across the planet.

Q. Is there water on Mars now?

A. Yes, patches of moisture have been detected in the soil. And NASA's InSight Lander has detected lots of water deep under the planet's crust. But we think that Mars was much wetter in the past than it is today.

Q. How do orbiters work? Can I hitch a lift?

A. Seven NASA orbiters orbit Mars, as of 2025. They are all unmanned.

It's not possible to hitch a lift to Mars … yet!

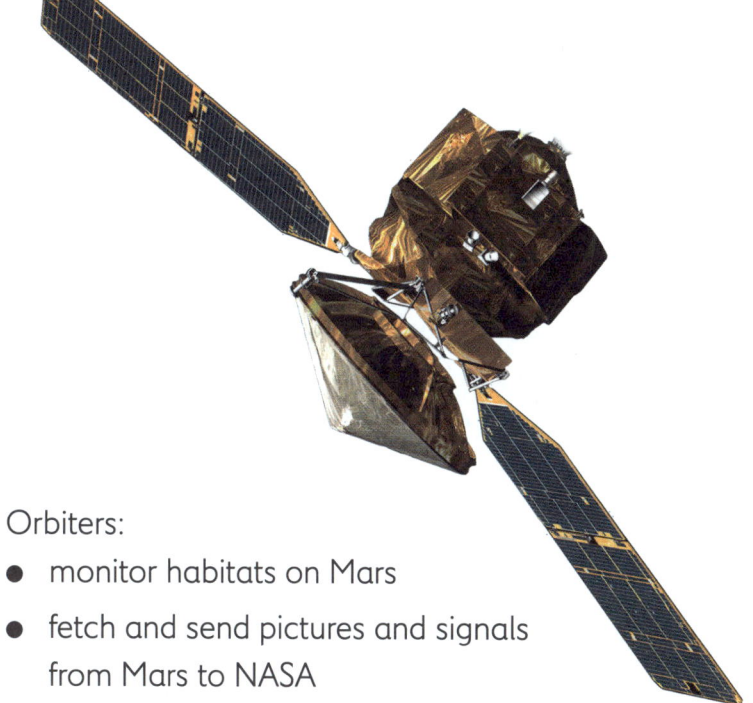

Orbiters:

- monitor habitats on Mars
- fetch and send pictures and signals from Mars to NASA
- help landers travel down to Mars.

Orbiters capture sunlight for power. They will orbit Mars for many years to come!

NASA has sent many landers to Mars. Just 50% have landed. Landing on Mars is complex. If the structure of the lander is knocked, it can crash.

Landing on Mars:
1) The roamer hitches a lift with the lander.
2) The lander ejects a hatch that frees the roamer.
3) Airbags protect the roamer.
4) Thrusters switch on. The lander aims for a patch clear of rocks.

Q. What might living on Mars be like?

A. The temperature on Mars is freezing. There is no air and lots of red dust. Your living habitat will have hatches and airlocks that keep air in and dust out. Your kitchen will stock food farmed on Mars in structures powered by the sun.

Exploring Mars will be an adventure. You might have a hover car to speed across the planet, looking for water!

Too Much Sugar

| /r/ wr | /w/ wh | /f/ ph |

| sugar | water | couldn't | would |

Too Much Sugar is a contemporary story.

Zac has a **knack** for tennis; he trains hard and his coach thinks he could be a star! But Zac starts to feel **wretched** – he is thirsty and needs the toilet all the time. His dad takes him to the doctors and he discovers that he has diabetes. Now Zac has to have a **sensor** to monitor his blood sugars and insulin injections to control his diabetes.

Zac feels there is an **elephant in the room**: no one wants to talk about how this affects his tennis dreams. He feels like a **wreck**: he hates having to monitor the **carbs** he eats and he feels he has no hope to shine at tennis. Then he sees his tennis hero on TV and everything changes ...

Vocabulary:
- **knack:** talent
- **wretched:** very unhappy
- **sensor:** a device to measure something
- **elephant in the room:** a problem that everyone knows but doesn't want to talk about
- **wreck:** unhealthy; tired
- **carbs:** carbohydrates; foods with sugars and starches

What would give you hope if you felt really down?

TOO MUCH SUGAR

Zac loved tennis, and he trained whenever possible. His coach was impressed with his strength and speed.

"You've got the knack for this! If you stretch yourself, you'll be a star," she said.

But soon after that, Zac started to feel ill. Just standing up knocked him out. He wanted to drink water all the time – but drinking didn't help. He kept needing the toilet.

"What's wrong?" his dad asked, as they sat in the kitchen having lunch. "You seem so …" He tailed off.

"I feel like a wreck," Zac said.

"I'll book a doctor's appointment," Dad responded.

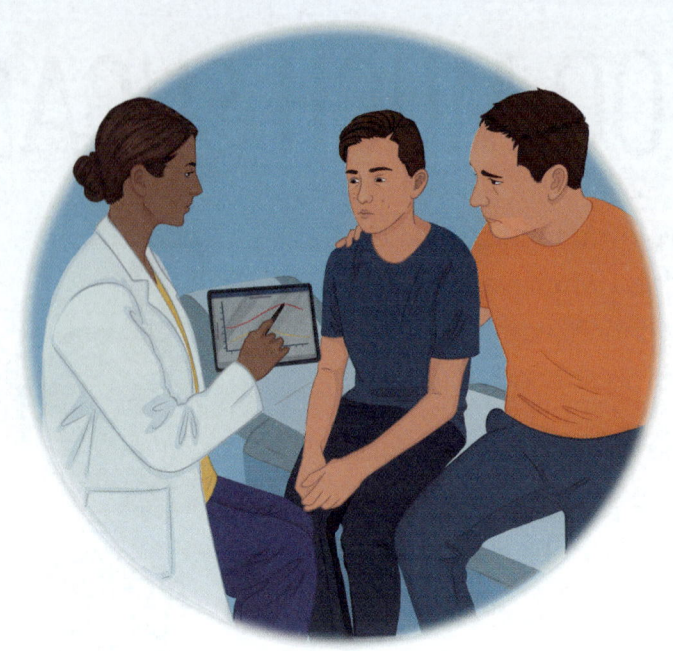

"Sharp scratch," the doctor said. She pricked Zac's finger then frowned.

"What's wrong?" asked Dad.

"When you look at this graph, you can see that the sugar levels in Zac's sample are too high," she said.

"I don't understand," Zac whispered.

The doctor explained that Zac had an illness, in which he struggled to convert the sugar from his food into power. This knocked him back and made him drink lots of water. "But you can inject a drug, which will put things right."

At the hospital, Zac couldn't help whimpering when they injected him. Being injected would be a constant thing from now on. He got a sensor, too, which would monitor his sugar levels.

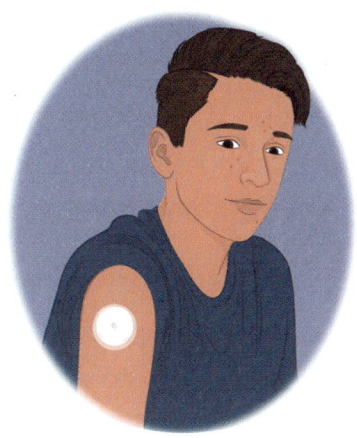

Zac felt wretched. He had to track the carbs in his food. Sweets had loads of carbs, so they sent his sugar levels too high. Dad wanted him to have good food, like chicken salad wraps. But Zac just wanted the sweets he shouldn't have.

The elephant in the room was that Zac couldn't picture himself as a tennis star now.

One afternoon, when Zac was very down, he turned on the TV. The tennis was on – Alexander Zverev was at match point. Zac was impressed with his incredible backhand.

Zac looked up Zverev and stumbled upon an article that said he needed to inject for his sugar levels, too. But that didn't stop him.

This spurred Zac to see his coach.

"I'm a bit of a wreck," he said. "My wrist is stiff from having so much time off. But I'm going to be a tennis star like Zverev."

Coach grinned. "Let's get training, then!"

The Squirrel that forgot to hide.

There was a rock, wood, tree and a river, but it's asking so much time for filtering into a rock but not water.

Don't give up! Keep on going!

Acknowledgements

The publishers gratefully acknowledge the permission granted to reproduce the copyright material in this book. Every effort has been made to trace copyright holders and to obtain their permission for the use of copyright material. The publishers will gladly receive any information enabling them to rectify any error or omission at the first opportunity.

p7 Zoonar GmbH/Alamy Stock Photo, p8 Helga_creates/Shutterstock, p11 geogphotos/Alamy Stock Photo, pp19–23 all images in photo collages: Shutterstock, p31 leolintang/Shutterstock, p32t hmorena/Shutterstock, p32b hmorena/Shutterstock, p33t hmorena/Shutterstock, p33b hmorena/Shutterstock, p34 hmorena/Shutterstock, p35 leolintang/Shutterstock, p45t Anton_Ivanov/Shutterstock, p45b Spencer Platt/Getty Images, p46t PA Images/Alamy Stock Photo, reproduced with permission from Bex Glover, Lucas Antics, Sophie Long, Gemma Compton, Ejits and Zoe Power, p46b Jui-Chi Chan/Alamy Stock Photo, p47t Mural artwork by rogueone, photo: Hemis/Alamy Stock Photo, p47b Gordon Saunders/Shutterstock, p48t Jon Bower/Alamy Stock Photo, p48b © 2025 Kobra/DACS, London, photo: Silvio Figueiredo/Alamy Stock Photo, p49 Keith Haring artwork © Keith Haring Foundation, photo: Associated Press/Alamy Stock Photo, p51 Ammit Jack/Shutterstock, p52t © Sam Toolsie 2023, p52b ZUMA Press, Inc./Alamy Stock Photo, p53 Sam Mellish/Alamy Stock Photo, p54t AFP/Getty Images, p54b Alan Dawson/Alamy Stock Photo, p55 Marco Ciccolella/Shutterstock, p57 alexkoral/Shutterstock, p58t Siberian Art/Shutterstock, p58b Tomasz Skoczen/Getty Images, p59 vikiss/Shutterstock, p60 IHelly/Shutterstock, p61t bsd studio/Shutterstock, p61b aopsan/Shutterstock, p77 MudaCom/Shutterstock, p78 VectorMine/Shutterstock, p79t adike/Shutterstock, p79b Boiling1/Creative Commons Attribution-Share Alike 4.0 International, p80t kakteen/Shutterstock, p80bl Eric Isselee/Shutterstock, p80br Eric Isselee/Shutterstock, p81 MudaCom/Shutterstock, p89 NASA, p91 NASA.

Published by Collins
An imprint of HarperCollins*Publishers*
The News Building, 1 London Bridge Street, London, SE1 9GF, UK

HarperCollins*Publishers*
Macken House, 39/40 Mayor Street Upper, Dublin 1, D01 C9W8, Ireland

Browse the complete Collins catalogue at
collins.co.uk

© HarperCollins*Publishers* Limited 2026

Wandle Learning Trust name and logo © Wandle Learning Trust

10 9 8 7 6 5 4 3 2 1

A catalogue record for this publication is available from the British Library.

ISBN 978-0-00-879094-3

All rights reserved. No part of this publication may be reproduced, stored in a retrieval system, or transmitted in any form by any means, electronic, mechanical, photocopying, recording or otherwise, without the prior written permission of the Publisher or a licence permitting restricted copying in the United Kingdom issued by the Copyright Licensing Agency Ltd, 5th Floor, Shackleton House, 4 Battle Bridge Lane, London SE1 2HX.

Without limiting the exclusive rights of any author, contributor or the publisher of this publication, any unauthorised use of this publication to train generative artificial intelligence (AI) technologies is expressly prohibited. HarperCollins also exercise their rights under Article 4(3) of the Digital Single Market Directive 2019/790 and expressly reserve this publication from the text and data mining exception.

Authors: Caroline Green, Jacqueline Harris, Emily Hooton, Charlotte Raby, Abbie Rushton, Rachel Russ, Jonny Walker and Clare Helen Welsh
Illustrators: Chiara Fedele (Astound US), Sylwia Filipczak (Advocate Art), Zoë Hansen (Advocate Art), Douglas Lopes (Illo Agency), Wan Norazura (Astound US), János Orban (Beehive Illustration), Jonas Pina (Astound US), Gaby Verdooren (Advocate Art), Laszlo Veres (Beehive Illustration) and Lilitt Wang (Advocate Art)
Publisher: Katie Sergeant
Product manager: Natasha Paul
Education consultant: Charlotte Raby
Project manager: Emily Hooton
Phonics reviewers: Catherine Baker and Abbie Rushton
Proofreader and fact checker: Catherine Dakin
Cover designer: Sarah Finan
Cover images: Catmando/Shutterstock and The Picture Art Collection/Alamy (background)
Internal designer: 2Hoots Publishing Services Ltd
Production controller: Sophie Waeland

Developed in collaboration with Wandle Learning Trust

Printed in the UK by Martins the Printers

MIX
Paper | Supporting responsible forestry
FSC™ C013254

Made with responsibly sourced paper and vegetable ink

Scan to see how we are reducing our environmental impact.

Collins would like to thank Abi Rothe, Nicola Dickens and the schools involved in the Code pilot for contributing to the development of this book.

Access the planning and resources to teach this book at littlewandlecode.org.uk